Harvey's Wish

Story by Matthew Fitzgerald
Illustrations by Jean Pidgeon

RSVP
RAINTREE
Steck-Vaughn
PUBLISHERS
The Steck-Vaughn Company

Austin, Texas

To my family, for all their love and support. — M.F.

To Aunt Helen, with love. — J.P.

Library of Congress Cataloging-in-Publication Data

Fitzgerald, Matthew, 1985-
    Harvey's wish / story by Matthew Fitzgerald; illustrations by Jean Pidgeon.
      p.   cm. — (Publish-a-book)
    Summary: Although Harvey starts out on a sunny morning, by the time he has finished helping his neighbors, it does not look as though he will be able to enjoy a day at the beach.
    ISBN 0–8114–7271-X
    1. Children's writings, American.   [1. Ants — Fiction. 2. Insects — Fiction.   3. Neighborliness — Fiction. 4. Friendship — Fiction.   5. Children's writings.] I. Pidgeon, Jean, ill. II. Title.   III. Series. PZ7.F57536Har   1995
[Fic] — dc20
                                  94-39154
                                  CIP   AC

Harvey the ant had been thinking about something for quite a while. "Oh, how I wish the sun would come out. I can't wait to go to the beach." Harvey had been waiting all winter to be able to sit in the hot sun and frolic in the cool waves of the ocean.

One night, before Harvey went to bed, he looked out his window and saw the first star of the night. "Oh, how I wish it would be sunny tomorrow so that I could spend time at the beach." He went to bed and dreamed of the warm sun and the smell of the ocean.

The next morning, Harvey was up before it was light out. He packed his little bag with his favorite new book, a bottle of sunscreen, his sunglasses, and a bottle of spring water. Then he sat, and he sat, waiting to see if the sun would come up.

Hooray! At last! The sky turned a beautiful deep blue and the sun was rising. Harvey was so excited. He grabbed his little bag with all the necessary items for a day at the beach and walked out into the sunlight. Ah, what a day he was going to have!

On his front porch, he grabbed his little beach chair, put on his sunglasses and his little straw hat, and headed for the beach.

He had walked for quite a while when he saw his friend Sam the caterpillar trying to get his car started.

"Hey, Harvey!" Sam yelled. "Where are you off to?"

Harvey yelled back, "I'm on my way to the beach! What seems to be the trouble?"

"I wish I knew what the trouble was. I'm supposed to start my vacation today, but now I guess I'll have to spend all day working on this car."

Harvey thought for a moment. It was still quite early. He could help his friend Sam get his car going and still have plenty of time to lie out on the beach. He told Sam what he thought might be the trouble, and an hour later the engine was running fine.

"Thanks, Harvey. You really are a good friend. Thanks for taking time out to help me."

"No problem, but let me get going. I can't wait to get on the beach." He waved good-bye to his friend and started off down the road. He still had a good way to go, but that didn't bother him. His wish had come true. He was on his way to the beach.

Harvey walked on and on. He came to Grandma Ladybug's house. She was sitting on the front porch in her favorite rocking chair.

"Hi, Grandma Ladybug. How are you this lovely sunny day?"

"Oh, I'm just fine, my boy. What are you up to so early in the morning?"

"I'm on my way to the beach."

"Well, isn't that nice." She tried to rock on her chair, but it wouldn't budge.

"Hmm," thought Harvey, "she doesn't look so fine to me."

"What seems to be the trouble with your chair?" he asked.

"Well, dearie, I'm not quite sure. I woke up this morning and came out to enjoy the sun, and my rocker seems to be broken. Oh, how I wish I could fix it, but I am an old ladybug and I'm afraid there are a few things I just can't do."

Harvey thought for a moment. Now, how long could it take to fix the rocking chair? Besides, he still had plenty of time to get to the beach.

An hour later Grandma Ladybug was rocking contentedly on her porch. "Oh, thank you, Harvey." She gave him a big hug. "You're such a sweet boy. Now, run along! Have a good time at the beach."

Harvey waved good-bye and started down the road. He still had a good way to go. He started to whistle. Yep, he was happy. He was on his way to the beach.

He had been walking for a while when he passed his friend Louie the grasshopper. "How are you?" he asked Louie.

"Not so good," Louie said. "I got this piano this morning, and now I can't seem to get it up the stairs and into the doorway. I wish I could figure this out. My brother is here to help, but we just can't seem to make it work." Then he noticed Harvey's beach chair. "Off to the beach? I know how much you love it."

Harvey thought for a moment. He wasn't that far from the beach now. Anyway, how long could it take for him to help out his good friend Louie?

Two hours later, the piano was sitting in Louie's living room. "Thanks a lot, Harv. You are truly a good friend. You better hurry, though. It doesn't look as sunny as it did before." Sure enough, a few clouds had started gathering in the sky. But that didn't bother Harvey.

"No problem," he said, "I've got plenty of time." He waved to his friend and hurried down the road.

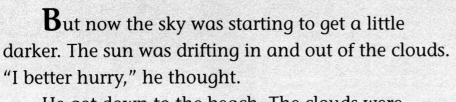

But now the sky was starting to get a little darker. The sun was drifting in and out of the clouds. "I better hurry," he thought.

He got down to the beach. The clouds were starting to thicken. He opened up his chair, put some sunscreen on, sat down, and opened his book. "Well," he thought excitedly, "I'm finally here." He sat back, and as he did so, he felt a drop of rain on his nose.

"Oh, no," he thought. "I guess it just wasn't meant to be." Sadly, he folded up his little chair and packed up his little bag. He started back up the road to his house. On the way, he passed his friend Louie.

"Hey, Harvey! I'm so sorry I messed up your day. Look, we had a little barbecue, and this is for you." He held out a platter with a nice juicy steak and some potatoes.

"Well, thank you, Louie."

16

Harvey started up the road and passed Grandma Ladybug's house. "Well, I was hoping to see you, my boy. This is for you, for all your help." She handed him a little box with a luscious strawberry shortcake inside.

"Hmm, my favorite. Thank you, Grandma. Good-bye," said Harvey.

She waved to him as he started up the road.

When Harvey got home, he put his beach chair away. By the door was a tall package. He opened it up. Inside was a sun lamp with a little note attached:

Dear Harvey,
    I felt so bad when I saw it starting to rain. If you hadn't stopped to help me, you probably would have had some time on the beach. Here you go, ol' buddy. I hope you can use this.

                Your friend,
                Sam

Harvey took the lamp inside. He set the lamp up and spread out his little beach chair. He took the platter with the steak and potatoes and the box with the cake in it and put them on the little table next to his chair. He turned on the lamp. My, how bright and warm it was! He spread a little sunscreen on his arms and face and sat down in his chair.

"Well," he thought to himself, "I guess I got my wish after all." He unpacked the platter and started to eat.

Matthew Fitzgerald, the author of **Harvey's Wish**, has an active imagination that serves him well. As a second-grade student at St. Cecilia School in Rockaway, New Jersey, Matthew was sponsored in the 1994 Young Publish-a-Book Contest by Mrs. Suzanne Pangallo, the school librarian.

Matthew's home is in Rockaway with his parents, John, a telecommunications technician, and Kate, a telemarketing researcher. He has two younger sisters, Stephanie and Corrinne. Matthew started telling the story of Harvey to his sisters at night as a bedtime story. All the characters and their "wishes" come directly from incidents at home and from his experiences with friends and relatives.

Matthew loves to be outside playing, especially hockey or soccer, but his favorite pastime is playing his computer games. His favorite subjects in school are math and science (not English!).

When asked if he wants to make a career out of writing, he says that it's too soon to tell, feeling that he may want to become an astronaut or a firefighter instead. For now, he'll just keep putting his thoughts on paper and wait to see what the future will bring.

The ten honorable-mention winners in the **1994 Raintree/Steck-Vaughn Young Publish-a-Book Contest** were Maria Morris, Demmitt Elementary, Vandalia, Ohio; Gillian McHale, Bucks County Library Center, Doylestown, Pennsylvania; Kristen Passanisi, Naper Elementary School, Naperville, Illinois; Erin Renzas, DePortola School, Mission Viejo, California; Hannah Mahuta, Fox River Christian Academy, Waukesha, Wisconsin; Lakeshe Ann Cephus, Lisbon Elementary, Waterproof, Louisiana; Brydey Redmon, H. B. Anderson Elementary, Garden Grove, California; Brittani Calmes, St. Mary's School, Colby, Wisconsin; Michelle Clark, DePortola School, Mission Viejo, California; Katie Lanning, Christ the King School, Dallas, Texas.

Jean Pidgeon lives in Maryland, on Bodkin Creek, along the Chesapeake Bay. She works at Historic Savage Mill, a renovated cotton mill that is now an antique and arts center. She loves every minute she spends making her living doing illustration for children and is thankful for all the wonderful writers who create a need for her work. Jean also illustrated *Friends Afloat*, the 1992 Raintree/Steck-Vaughn Young Publish-a-Book Contest winner.